CURVEBALLS

Curveballs

Written by

Alexandria Rose Fortier

Edited by

Jessica Jutras

Based on the novel Curveballs *by*

Catherine Mardon

First Printing: 2021

Cover Design and typeset by Clare Dalton

ISBN 978-1-77369-670-6

E-book ISBN 978-1-77369-671-3

Golden Meteorite Press

103 11919 82 St NW

Edmonton, AB T5B 2W3

www.goldenmeteoritepress.com

Curveballs

Written By: Alexandria Rose Fortier

Edited by Jessica Jutras

Based on the novel *Curveballs* by Catherine Mardon

2021

Characters

Catherine

Colonel

Father Paul

FBI Jones

Henchmen

Attacker

Cleaning Lady

Saving Grace

Sister Anne

ACT ONE

SCENE ONE

Lights out, a vacuum can be heard in the darkness. The lights slowly begin to rise in a single spot light on a lifeless body centre stage. Suddenly the woman vacuuming sees the body and screams. She runs off stage. The lights are fully up now. She returns with another woman, the first is still screaming. The new woman falls to her hands and knees to check the woman's pulse.

Woman 2:   There's a pulse. Quick go call an ambulance.

The cleaning lady runs off stage again.

Woman 2:   Stay with me. You're okay now,
stay with me.

The woman on the floor covered in blood tries to speak but you can't make out the words.

Woman 2:   I can't hear you. You've got to
stay with me.

The woman tries to speak again. This time woman 2 places her ear next to her lips to better hear her. She is now covered in the woman's blood. She understands what the woman is saying and begins to pray with her.

Woman 2:   It's okay now, I've got you. I hear you. I'll
pray for you now. Rest.

"Our Father who art in Heaven, Hallowed be His name."

She continues to pray and hold the woman. The lights begin to fade out and the siren of an ambulance can be heard growing louder as if it is getting closer with each word of prayer.

Black Out.

SCENE TWO

Start in black out. A voice can be heard in the darkness.

V.O.:   In life, you either learn how to throw the curveball, or you have to learn to hit one. This is a story about the person I was, the person I couldn't help becoming, and the person I strive to be now.

Lights slowly raise as if someone is opening their eyes for the first time in a long while. The woman is in a Hospital Bed and a Priest sits at the end of her bed, head on her legs, hands together in prayer. The woman is waking up and has no idea what has happened.

Catherine: Father Paul?

Ft. Paul: Catherine. My girl, you've scared me to death.

Catherine: Where am I?

Ft. Paul: You've been in a horrible accident my girl. You're in the hospital.

Catherine begins to get agitated now and tries to sit up. Machines start to make loud angry noises.

Catherine: I…I don't understand. Where am I? What happened to me, Father Paul. What happened to me?

Ft. Paul: Catherine, You need to calm down. Lay back, it's alright. They can't hurt you anymore, you're safe.

Catherine: What's happened to me?!

Catherine is irate now. There is no consoling her. A nurse runs into the room and helps Father Paul Restrain her while a Doctor comes into the room with a needle to sedate her.

Ft. Paul: Rest now, the Lord will keep watch.

SCENE THREE

Father Paul is in an argument with two FBI agents outside of Catherine's hospital room.

Ft. Paul: I am telling you Special Agent Jones she doesn't remember anything. Haven't you put her through enough?

Jones: With all due respect Father, she is a leading witness in a federal terrorism investigation. We need her.

Ft. Paul: We all need her. She isn't a pawn to be pushed around on your quest for a checkmate. She is a living breathing human being, and she is now fighting for her life just steps away from you now. Do you have no compassion?

Jones: We didn't put her in that bed. She was in it before we ever even picked her up.

Ft. Paul: You may not have been the one to put the knife in her, but have no doubt that she is here as a direct cause and effect of your actions. Now please leave.

Jones: We'll be back.

Ft. Paul: I'm sure you will. Next time, maybe remember to bring some compassion and humanity.

The FBI agents exit and Father Paul stands his ground protecting Catherine's door.

SCENE FOUR

There are open desks everywhere and the noise of a busy office fills the stage. Catherine with a box in her arms follows an older woman to her new desk.

Co-Worker: We really can't tell you how excited we are to have you with us. The addition of a lawyer to our ranks is really going to make a big difference, HUGE! So, thank you so much. It's a little bit of learning on the fly around here, so sorry for that.

Her phone already begins to ring. She looks at it and looks at her co-worker who looks at her then at the phone.

Catherine: Oh!

She answers the phone.

Co-Worker: Good luck!

She stares at Catherine with a big grin until she answers the phone. Gives her a thumbs up and toddles off when she picks up the receiver.

Catherine: Hi there, you've reached the Farmers Home Administration, Catherine speaking.

Jeff: Hello?

Catherine: Hello?

Jeff: Are you the lawyer?

Catherine: Yes…and you are?

Jeff: Jeff. Sorry Ma'am. You see I'm just in a
bind here, I'm about to lose my farm, and I just really can't have
that happen.

Catherine: Don't worry Jeff, I'm here to help.

Jeff: That's excellent news. You see, I need some
advice. Grandfather started this farm during the depression and
my Father kept it going during the War, I can't be the one to
lose it now.

Catherine: Let's see what we can do. Why don't we
start at the beginning shall we?

Jeff: It started when the Colonel showed up
one day, talking about how he could save our farm and get us a
tax break. He said he had loans for sale, and that they weren't
controlled by…

*The conversation begins to fade out as Catherine sits at her desk
taking notes and listening to Jeff intently.*

SCENE FIVE

A Church service is just finishing up and Catherine is mingling with the other parishioners. Father Paul approaches her.

Ft. Paul: Beautiful singing today Catherine, it's like having our very own angel in the room with us.

Catherine: Father Paul, you are too kind.

Ft. Paul: You know I cannot lie. Tell me, how is the new job going?

They take a seat in one of the pews.

Catherine: Well it's quite interesting really. I didn't think it would be this challenging, yet as it goes there seems to be something nefarious going on, on these farms it seems. Or perhaps I mean, someone nefarious.

Ft. Paul: What have you stumbled into?

Catherine: That's just the thing, I have no idea. So far it just seems like a man with very terrible advice but a charming personality has been able to convince a lot of farmers to distrust the government and the federal banks and instead take loans out with him that are in fact the actual problem for these farmers in the grand picture. I don't know completely yet, I'm still trying to put it all together. I have a farmer, Jeff, who is trying to get me in contact with this man. They call him the Colonel. He's a hard man to get in touch with.

Ft. Paul: It sounds like you have quite the mystery on your hands, Catherine.

Catherine: Not so much a mystery, as a puzzle with a few missing pieces. Good news is, all puzzles are meant to be solved.

Ft. Paul: Just be careful. Don't go putting your nose where it shouldn't be.

Catherine: I can't make any promises I don't intend on keeping, Father Paul.

Ft. Paul: Lord give me strength so I can better guide
all your children.

They laugh it off as they stand to exit the church.

SCENE SIX

Father Paul sits at an interrogation table with FBI agent Jones.

Ft. Paul: Look, I've already told you everything I
believe to be helpful. Yes Catherine confided in me about The
Farm and the Colonel. But I don't know much of what she saw
or experienced first hand. She was terrified towards the end. All I
know is the threats never stopped. Not after she testified, not after
she moved. She was always looking over her shoulder. I mean she
left the church. She said it was for our protection, whatever
that truly means.

Jones: We are sorry for how all this turned out, but
without Catherine's memory returning there is not much we can
do about getting her justice, or having her original testimony even
stand up in court now.

Ft. Paul: You can't be serious. You're telling me that all this, everything she did and sacrificed was for nothing?

Jones: I take no pleasure in any of this.

Ft. Paul: Have you at the very least caught t he man responsible?

BEAT

Jones: There are no other eye witnesses, and Catherine can't give an accurate description of the assailant.

Ft. Paul: So what now?

Jones: We retrace our steps, to the beginning. And we pray for Catherine's recovery, including that of her memory.

Ft. Paul: Until then?

Jones: Pray.

Jones slides back out of his chair pushing himself up off the table, while Father Paul sits there incredulous.

SCENE SEVEN

Catherine stands outside beneath a tree fumbling through her purse while she looks for her car keys. When a tall and ominous figure steps out from the shadows and begins a conversation with her.

Colonel: Watching the Sooners this evening?

Catherine: Well I mean, football is as close to a religion as it gets here in Oklahoma, and I am a God Fearing Woman.

The Colonel laughs at this response and gets closer to her. Standing shoulder to shoulder.

Colonel: If you ask me, their season is all down here from here.

Catherine: I'm not saying you're wrong, just...misinformed.

Colonel: I'm never misinformed. About anything.

Catherine: I guess only time will tell.

Colonel: So, Catherine. Have you kept up with your riflery?

Catherine: *(taken aback, but trying to hide her fear)* Yes, I love getting to a range. It's my version of meditation, I suppose.

Colonel: Good to hear it. You should come out to my farm this Saturday, then. I have a private range. For just close friends of mine. And Catherine, you are going to be a friend of mine, aren't you?

Catherine: I guess only time will tell.

Colonel laughs again.

Colonel: You are a…funny woman. Don't be late.

Catherine: How will I find it?

Colonel: Take the highway a few miles out, you can't miss it.

Catherine: Alright then.

Colonel: *(Walking away with his back to her)* Don't forget to bring that gun of yours. *BEAT.* Oh, and Catherine?

Catherine: Yes?

Colonel: Do make sure to come alone.

The Colonel exits off stage and a shiver runs down Catherine's spine. She stands there a moment before she comes too, and bolts off stage with a purpose.

SCENE EIGHT

Catherine enters a gun shop. A man stands behind the counter and watches her as she looks around.

Shop Owner:　　　　Can I help you, Miss?

Catherine:　　　　Yes, I'm looking for a target rifle.

Shop Owner:　　　　We have this beautiful hunting
rifle new in…

Catherine:　　　　I'm not looking for a hunting rifle, I need
a .22 caliber.

Shop Owner:　　　　Oh, I see. Follow me.

He leads her to a section clearly intended for children's starting rifles.

Catherine: I'm not shopping for a child, I'm shopping for myself.

Shop Owner: Then why are you after a children's rifle?

Catherine: Look, I used to shoot on my University Rifle team. I'm after a .22 because I'll be putting a lot of rounds through it, and, well, to be honest they are just cheaper. So I'd really appreciate it if you would cut the crap, and just get me what I asked for. *BEAT.* Please.

BEAT.

Shop Owner: Right this way, Ma'am. What you need is actually a high capacity .22. That is different.

Catherine: These look like they came from the set of Rambo.

Shop Owner: Beautiful, aren't they?

Catherine: I never believed in love at first sight 'till now.

He takes out a gun and hands it to her.

Shop Owner: It's a Ruger 10/22.

Catherine: I'll take it.

Shop Owner: Excellent choice. You'll also be needing these then.

The Shop Owner goes behind the counter and pulls out and slams down some large capacity clips. She nods and points out a case and the lights fade down as they chatter about the gun.

SCENE NINE

In a black out a voice is heard.

V.O.:   I went to the gun range every day that week. I knew I had to look as comfortable firing my new gun as I would holding my morning coffee. I didn't have the words for it then, but my body knew my life very well might depend on getting this right. So I took a deep breath, counted to three, and pulled the trigger.

BEAT.

One.

BEAT.

Two.

BEAT.

Three.

At three the gun fire goes off for several seconds. The stage remains dark only being lit up with shots fired. After a few beats it stops. The lights fade up as a whooshing sound of the target being reeled in is heard. Lights up on Catherine holding a perfect marked up target to the light. Beams spilling through the holes all perfectly centered.

SCENE TEN

Catherine stands outside an old cattle gate. She paces back and forth. It's chained. She's waiting for the Colonel. A man approaches, she startles a bit.

Catherine: Hello?

Henchmen: Catherine. Follow me.

Catherine: Who are you?

Henchmen: Colonel sent me to bring you in.

Catherine: And where is the Colonel?

Henchmen: Waiting for you.

The Farm is completely empty, despite looking like it was recently just in use. She hears a distant rustling and stops to look around.

Henchmen: Please keep moving.

She runs to catch up to him. They enter a room that is a dining room. A large oak table with several chairs neatly tucked in. Six or so coffee cups are on the table in different levels of use. Some even have steam coming from them.

Catherine: Have I interrupted something?

Henchmen: No, please sit.

He exits off stage as Catherine pulls out a chair and stares at the coffee mugs. The Colonel enters and pulls out the seat at the head of the table a distance away from Catherine.

Colonel: Catherine, my dear, great to see you again. How have you been?

Catherine: Great, thank you for asking.

Colonel: So tell me, did you get your love of shooting from your father and brothers? As I understand it, they all served time in the military. Well, except your youngest brother.

Catherine: Yes, they did. I can honestly say they were the reason I joined the VFW Auxiliary. So, yes I suppose they have a hand in why I joined riflery in the beginning. Although, I think I would have found my way to it regardless.

Colonel: And why is that?

Catherine: I really like the feeling of /

Colonel: Pulling the trigger/ It's the power my dear. It becomes…addicting. Your youngest brother, how did he get out of the draft?

Catherine: He didn't. I mean, it's not how it sounds. His eighteenth birthday was just after the draft ended in '75. It wouldn't really have made a difference though. My Father told him that had he been drafted, he'd have been happy to smuggle him across the Canadian Border.

Colonel: Did he make that offer to your other brothers? They all served.

Catherine: No, he didn't.

Colonel: And why was that?

Catherine: I think it was largely because, by the time my brother turned eighteen, my Father had watched the war drag on for longer than it should have. He became rather disillusioned with the government and the way they handled the war in Vietnam. He just couldn't bring himself to support it any more.

The Colonel lets out a deep laugh and rubs his hands together. He stands.

Colonel: Catherine, would you like a tour?

He turns and walks off stage expecting to be followed.

SCENE ELEVEN

The Colonel and Catherine arrive at the gun range part of The Farm.

Colonel: And finally, the gun range.

Catherine: They had me leave my gun in the car back
at the gate.

Colonel: Don't worry about that, I had someone
bring it over.

Catherine: My gun?

Colonel: Yes. It's very well loved.

Catherine: That it is. Wasn't my car locked?

Colonel: No. Here it is now.

The German Henchmen enters carrying Catherine's rifle. She tries to hide her mounting unease.

Catherine: Thank you. I didn't get your name
at the gate.

Henchman: You don't need it.

Exits

Colonel: He's not very chatty.
(motions to targets) Shall we?

Catherine: Are you shooting as well?

Colonel: If it's all the same, I think I'll just
watch this round.

Catherine: If that is what you'd prefer.

Colonel: It is.

Catherine begins to inspect her gun and sets up. The Colonel watches her every move. She is finally satisfied and begins to aim and shoot. After a few rounds the target springs forward. Again, all perfectly centered shots, with one to the head. The Colonel shows very little.

Catherine: Not my best work, but not bad either. Shall we go another round?

Colonel: I think we are done for the day. Go ahead and clean your gun.

She begins to clean the gun and again the Colonel watches her every move. She finishes up and he nods. The Henchmen enters again and they whisper to each other. He walks over and takes the gun from Catherine.

Colonel: Don't worry, he will return it to your vehicle. Let's head back in. It's almost supper time and I don't know about you, but I've really worked up an appetite.

Again he begins walking away without looking back to see if he was indeed being followed.

SCENE TWELVE

They enter the dining room again. On the stove in the nearby kitchen you can see pots with chili being cooked and the table is fully set, but again, no one there besides the two of them.

Colonel: Have a seat Catherine, I just need to have a word with the chef and let him know we have one more joining us.

She takes a seat and he disappears around a corner. You can hear unclear mumbles from the direction he disappeared from and a loud crack rings out that causes Catherine to jump. The Colonel enters the room rubbing his hands together and begins clapping. At this sound a rush of people fill the space taking the empty seats all around Catherine. She tries to catch their conversations, some ordinary, some rambling conspiracies about the government. The cook begins to ladle out soup. As everyone began to eat, the conversation all but died out and a silence fell over the group as they ate. The Colonel breaks the silence.

Colonel: Earlier at the range, I noticed your rifle is drilled for a scope Catherine, but you didn't have one. Why's that?

Catherine: I used to use a scope, but I found it limited my field of vision and the ability to react to quickly changing situations.

Colonel: And I couldn't help but notice that when you cleaned your rifle, you used a coated nylon road, not a metal rod.

Catherine: I found that a coated nylon road is better for the barrel. It's less likely to scratch the inside, and therefore less dirt builds up in those cracks the rod leaves over time.

Colonel: I've never found this to be the case.

Everyone at the table has stopped eating and is watching this exchange. Catherine doesn't flinch.

Catherine: On anything bigger than a .22 I only use a stainless steel rod. But the thing with a .22 bore is it's such a tight fit that you run the risk of damaging the rifle in the bore.

The Colonel thinks a moment. Then stands without a word and walks over the a cabinet filled with rifles. He unlocks it and grabs half a dozen different sized rods. He drops them in front of Catherine who grabs one in her hands and wipes it clean. It doesn't come clean and she hands it to him pointing out the scratches. She picks another one up and says "Stainless Steel" and does the same. This comes out sparkly clean.

BEAT.

Colonel: Well I'll be damned. What kind of solvent do you use?

Catherine: I only use Hoppes #9. I have always loved the smell of it.

At this, the Colonel slammed his hands down at the table and started laughing.

Colonel: I have never met a woman who knew how to really clean a gun before, and here you are teaching me something new, and I've been shooting since I was old enough to hold one. I also love the smell of Hoppes. I hope you've enjoyed your time here Catherine, I'd very much like it if you'd make frequent visits out here to the Farm and join all of us.

Catherine: I have. Thank you for the invitation, I'd really like that.

SCENE THIRTEEN

It's the end of another church service and Catherine and Father Paul sit in a pew. They are in the middle of a conversation.

Catherine: I know I'm there undercover Father Paul, but I find myself starting to like the man a little more each time I go out to the farm.

Ft. Paul: Catherine, are you sure that this is safe?

Catherine: In all honesty, Father, I'm not sure. When I got home from my last visit, I noticed a handprint on my trunk. When I opened it, I noticed all my belongings had been moved around. Which makes sense since someone had to go in to get my gun. So I checked my glove compartment to see if anything in there had been moved.

Ft. Paul: And?

Catherine: Everything was out of order. They are definitely looking into me. He already knew so much about my family.

Ft. Paul: Listen to me, I don't think you should be going out there anymore.

Catherine: I need to go back. I'm so close to finding out what his scheme is. The sooner I find out how he's hoodwinking all these innocent farmers, the sooner I can stop going back there.

Ft. Paul: You know that I support you in all that you do, but this Catherine… I'm just not sure about it.

Catherine: I'll be careful, Father. I know this is something I need to do. It's for the greater good.

Ft. Paul: I know all about the greater good, Catherine, just please, I beg of you don't get so deep that you lose yourself or worse.

Catherine: I promise.

SCENE FOURTEEN

*In black out, the crashing noises of heart monitors flatlining can
be heard. Doctors screaming in code, Father Paul's voice ringing
out for Catherine to fight. Him saying he needs to do the last
rights before surgery. Catherine's disheveled voice trying to say
the Lord's Prayer. The first verse over and over again, three times
until it fades out in a whisper.*

SCENE FIFTEEN

*The Farm is buzzing. More people there than ever before. The
German Henchman has one hand on Catherine's arm and is
"guiding" her through the crowd.*

Catherine: You're hurting me. Please let me go.

Henchmen: The Colonel wants to see you right away. Doesn't want you getting…lost.

Catherine: I am a grown woman, I think I grasped the concept of following when I was two.

She yanks back her arm which enrages the Henchmen who steps close to her face and is about to scream at her when the Colonel appears clapping and rubbing his hands together at the sight of her.

Colonel: Catherine, my dear. You made it in one piece. How lovely to see you again.

Catherine: Are you having a party?

Colonel: No, no. Well, yes. I guess you could say it's a bit of a party. You picked a lovely day to join us. Come in, come in. I have some big news for you.

Catherine side steps the Henchmen glaring at him as she passes and enters the same kitchen area as the first time she arrived at the farm. There are a few people around the table, she waves to them, more familiar with them now. She takes her usual seat.

Catherine: What sort of big news do you have for me?

Colonel: Well my dear, it's more of a favour. As I'm sure you're aware by now, I have been doing my due diligence and checking into you.

Catherine: Have you?

Colonel: Don't play coy with me, Catherine, you've known since our first meeting under the tree. I've been checking in, because I do hope we can be friends. Do you consider us to be friends, Catherine?

Catherine: *(Nervous and caught off guard)* I'd like to think so, Sir.

Colonel: Are you someone that I can depend on, Catherine?

Catherine: I hope so.

Colonel: I hope so too, my dear. For both our sakes. You puzzle me, Catherine. You grew up in the city, but studied agriculture. You're a woman, but can shoot as well as any man I have ever met. You're Catholic, apparently a devout one by the amount of time you spend at Church with Father Paul, and yet, you work alongside Protestants without trying to convert them. You're obviously bright as a whip but you have asked me very few questions in all our time together these last three months. People who don't ask questions in my experience are either too dumb to or they already know the answers.

The Colonel stares down Catherine, there is a heat before she collects herself enough to respond. She knows this is a do or die situation.

Catherine: I only studied agriculture because they made me. I majored in forestry. That's in the Ag Department. If it had been in the Science department, I wouldn't have taken a single agricultural course. I have always loved being in the woods. I don't know why it is that I'm such a good shot. My father earned his marksmanship badge in the army so maybe it is genetic, or maybe, and what I like to assume, it's a lot of hard work and perseverance. The willingness to sacrifice everything to be the best. You can't just want to be the best at something, that's only half of it. The rest is earned in the hours and the sacrifices it takes to become the best. I think I've always been pretty good at things I like because I put that effort into them. I don't convert people because talking about religion always leads to fights, and that touchy-feely stuff kind of makes me uncomfortable. Now, as for the questions. If I don't ask many questions, maybe it's because as a lawyer I have learned that there are some I just don't want to know the answers to.

There is a long beat as The Colonel takes in Catherine's answers.

Colonel: In the work I do, I am surrounded by people who just tell me what they think I want to hear. You don't do that. You tell people the truth even when it makes you look bad. The reason I first approached you is because a farmer I respect told me that he asked you something, and that you admitted you didn't know the answer, but you would try and find out for him, and you did just that. I have never known any doctors or lawyers or military officers who were willing to admit that they didn't know something. Brutal honesty and intelligence don't usually go hand in hand. What I need is someone to tell me the truth even when I don't want to hear it.

BEAT

Catherine: I don't know what you're asking of me. I'm not sure what is exactly going on here. I get invited to a lot of farms by my clients, usually for barbeques or weddings, and sometimes unfortunately for foreclosure auctions. Yet, I haven't seen any farming going on here. Not a tractor, or a row to sow. I don't know what it is you want from me, Sir.

The Colonel inhales sharply and jumps to his feet crossing the room to pour himself a cup of coffee. He takes his time as he goes. When he finally sits back down is when he speaks.

Colonel: I need some help with government paperwork. I need someone I can trust, and you Catherine, have been recommended by every person that I have asked. *(BEAT)* I'm being sued by the government. I can't find an attorney to represent me in the way that I want to be represented. I want to use my time in court to make the government prove that they have the right to even ask me to be present. I served this country proudly, and it hurts me to see how it has lost its way. Many of my friends have stopped paying their taxes. I have surrendered my driver's license. I do not put a tag on my truck. They don't have the right to ask me to. They lost that right when they turned the government over to the Jews. I want to be a completely sovereign citizen, not a fourteenth amendment citizen. I am subject only to the common law passed down to us by our white ancestors. What I want you to help me with is, I want to be completely redeemed from the U.S. Government. You may not realize this, but they enslaved us all by using us as collateral for foreign debt. I need you to help me fill out the forms I need to free myself. I want to be completely free and sovereign from this government so they no longer have the right to take my farm away from me.

BEAT.

BEAT.

BEAT.

BEAT.

BEAT.

Catherine: I have never heard of the U.S. citizens being considered as collateral for debt. This is all really new information for me. I'd have to review your paperwork and look all this up before I can make any type of commitment to draw up any paperwork on your behalf. I would also need to clear this kind of casework with my Director to make sure that he will even allow me to work on it, since it would be way outside my regular duties.

Colonel: That seems more than reasonable. Now, why don't you come with me? There are some people I'd like you to meet.

A shaky and unnerved Catherine steels herself as she stands and follows The Colonel off stage.

SCENE SIXTEEN

Inside a large army tent there are rows and rows of people awaiting The Colonel's arrival and they all begin to hoot and cheer when he walks in with Catherine. To stage right, there are massive ammunition boxes being loaded out to be "STORED." The Henchmen appears again and tries to wrap his hand around Catherine's arm but she swats him away.

Colonel: Hello, everyone. Thank you for coming out, we do, in fact, have cause to celebrate. I would like to introduce you all to a very special woman. Some of you already have the great fortune to know her as she's become quite the regular here at our gun range, and for some of you this will be your first introduction. I'd like you to meet Catherine, she is my new lawyer friend from the Ag. Coalition. She's the one your lawyers call when they don't know something. She's been getting to know us, and is trying to decide if she is able to help us put together redemption packets. She's one of the good guys. Even if she is Catholic. We'll have to work on that later. *(crowd roars with laughter and he slaps a hand on Catherine's shoulder.)* She will be getting familiar with our operations over the coming weeks so that she will be better able to meet our legal needs. And we have lots of those my friends.

The Colonel's speech begins to become almost static. We can see he is still pandering to the crowd but the words become indistinguishable. Catherine begins to wobble unsteadily. She turns to the Henchmen.

Catherine: I'm sorry, I have to go. I'm terribly claustrophobic.

Catherine rushes off stage.

SCENE SEVENTEEN

Catherine is at lunch. She is sitting alone at a table when a woman sits down with her and begins to eat.

JONES: I don't want to cause a scene here. *(Carries on pretending to eat)* I need to know if you will cause one. We can do this the easy way, or we can do this the hard way. The choice is completely up to you.

Catherine looks up from her plate, at FBI agent Jones then over each shoulder.

Catherine: I beg your pardon. Are you speaking to me?

FBI agent Jones finally makes direct eye contact with Catherine.

JONES: I have back up outside, I just don't want to make our presence too visible. You and I, we need to have a conversation. Now, you can comply and follow me out the door and we can be on our way, or we can take you out of here in handcuffs. If you are willing to go peacefully, we will sit here and finish our lunches, then you will hand me your keys and I will have someone drive your car to our office and you can ride with me.

Catherine: I'm still lost. What is it you even want with me? I haven't done anything.

JONES: Miss Reilly, you are an officer of the court. You are required to cooperate with law enforcement. I want to know if you are going to do so.

Catherine: Of course I am. I just want to know what it is you want from me.

JONES: We will discuss that later. Now I suggest you finish your lunch as it will be a while before either of us will be seeing anything more than crappy office coffee.

Catherine sits staring at her lunch. She shakes her head as if coming back into her body and finishes up her lunch. She stands, quietly slipping her car keys on the table as she walks over to the trash bin to discard her tray. When she turns to leave she notices that Agent Jones has already left and her keys are gone. She takes a deep steadying breath and exits.

SCENE EIGHTEEN

Inside the same interview room as the one Father Paul was in earlier. Jones and Catherine sit opposite each other. Another FBI agent is a witness.

Jones: Before we start, I would like you to read this card and sign it at the bottom.

Catherine: This is a Miranda waiver card…

Jones: That's right, Miss Reilly.

Catherine: I'm certainly willing to sign this, because I have nothing to hide, but before I do, I want to know what is going on here.

Jones: We would like to ask you some questions about what it is you've been up to over at Bill Davidson's property.

Catherine: Bill Davidson?

Jones: Right. I believe people refer to
him as The Colonel.

Catherine: This is about The Colonel?

Jones: At present you are not being
investigated for anything other than having an extremely
poor choice in friends.

Catherine: He's not a friend. I've got enough crazy
friends without adding him to the mix.

*Jones nods at the card on the table in front of Catherine, who
signs it and slides it back across the table. Jones picks it up,
making sure she really signed it.*

Jones: I understand that you are an attorney, but
you do have the right to request one yourself to be present during
questioning. Are you willing to speak to us today
without one present?

Catherine: I haven't done anything wrong, Agent Jones, so please, feel free to ask me anything you like.

Jones: Glad to hear it, Miss Reilly. Next, I have a waiver here allowing us to search your vehicle. Since you have nothing to hide…

Jones slides another document across the table which Catherine happily signs for her.

Catherine: Full disclosure. In my trunk you will find a rifle. It is properly secured with a trigger lock and is unloaded.

Jones: We are aware of the Ruger in your trunk, Catherine.

Jones holds up a photo of Catherine placing the gun in her trunk.

Catherine: And why exactly is it, Agent Jones, that you have been taking pictures of me?

Agent Jones stands and walks over the two way mirror and debates how much information to give to Catherine.

Jones: We have spent the last couple of weeks turning your life inside-out. You make no sense to me. You work for a non-profit when you could easily be making a six figure salary as a litigator. The attorneys we talked to said you were the nicest person they knew, that is until you entered the courtroom. I understand you even made a judge cry once, yet you spend all your free time either volunteering at church or legal aid or the homeless shelter. You don't date /

Catherine: I da/

Jones: You don't date. You don't have any vices except expensive clothing, that we can find at least. Every person we have asked about you, have said the same thing, that you are just as you seem to be. So explain to me this, why on God's green earth do you spend half your weekends hanging out with serious scumbags?

Catherine: Thank you for that riveting assessment of my personal life, Agent Jones.

Jones: Don't get cute with me, just answer the question.

Catherine: Why I choose to spend my
time with scumbags?

Jones: Seriously, Catherine.
Help fill in the puzzle here.

Catherine: It's not by choice, if that's what you're
after. Well, that's a lie, it was my choice, but not for company
sake. When I first started at FmHA, I heard from one of my
farmers about a man who was offering truly terrible legal advice.
It had cost a few farmers their livelihoods, and one even their own
life. He was so in debt with no way out, and the banks coming to
repossess the land that had been in his family for generations that
the only thing he knew to do was suspend himself from a rope in
his barn. That kind of misinformation is treacherous. I couldn't
stand to think of one more good and hard working soul falling
prey to such evil.

Jones: Let me get this straight, you're telling me
that you're undercover?

Catherine: In a way, yes, I suppose that is how what
I'm doing could be described.

Jones: *(Jones puts a hand to her mouth and laughs out loud)* I'm sorry, it's just we have been trying to get a man on the inside for over two years. And you just walked right in. Within a couple of months. Does anyone else know about this? Do you have any sort of back up?

Catherine: Father Paul at my church is the only other living soul who knows. Besides the three of us in this room, and who's ever listening behind that mirror.

Jones laughs again.

Jones: You are lucky to be alive right now. You understand that much, correct?

Catherine: I understood every single risk I was taking when I entered that farm. There is no reason to talk down to me like I'm a twelve year old who took a spill off a swing seat. Especially since I've apparently accomplished something not even a single person in your entire organization could pull off in over two years.

Jones: *(Stills her laughter)* Forgive me, I didn't mean to insinuate…

Catherine: But you did. Now, if we are quite finished here?

Jones: Would you be willing to serve as our woman on the inside?

Catherine: As you have just so keenly pointed out, Agent Jones, I am lucky enough to be alive without getting myself further tangled up with the FBI.

Jones: Will you at least take some time to consider?

Catherine: Yes.

Jones: Great. Thank you for your cooperation here today, Miss Reilly. Please keep us informed of any further engagements you have planned with The Colonel.

Catherine: I am supposed to attend one of his rallies this weekend.

Jones: Perfect. We look forward to the potential of a partnership with you.

They stand, Jones stretches out her hand for a handshake. Catherine politely accepts before exiting the room.

SCENE NINETEEN

Catherine enters a giant rally. People with anti-government signs are everywhere. She settles into the back of the crowd just as the crowd erupts in cheers as The Colonel takes his place at the podium on the stage.

Colonel: Thank you all so very much for coming out today. I like to think of myself as a man of the people, by the people, for the people. *(crowd cheers)* I take on that role very seriously, taking your wellbeing and making it my top priority. Unlike our so-called government. *(More thunderous cheers)* I went to war for this country, I sweat and I bled for this country. Only to come home to have the very land I fought for threatened to be seized by the country I would have died for. Now tell me, does that sound fair to you?

The crowd is eating up every word The Colonel speaks.

Colonel:	Well I'm not going to stand for it. I encourage you all to do the same. Not as hard working American citizens, but as hard working men and women who have had enough of being sold at auction like a prize bull to the greedy Jews who've scratched and clawed their way into our country. If the United States of America has fallen into the money hungry, blood thirsty grips of second rate Kikes, then I no longer want to be counted as an American. And with that, I refused to hand over another penny to these monsters. So where do you start to take back what is rightly yours? Start here and now. Stop all payments on your VA loans immediately. The government can cover them. Take a final stand for your land, for your family. It's time to take back what they've been stealing from you.

The crowd goes wild. The German Henchmen chants out a Hitler manifesto cry. The Colonel makes his way through the adoring crowd with his Henchmen and greets Catherine.

Colonel:	It's electric isn't it?

Catherine:	It's…something.

Colonel:	Tell me that didn't move you to the very core, Catherine.

Catherine: It did.

Colonel: We can be unstoppable now that you're
on our team.

Catherine: I'm not.

Colonel: I'm sorry, I didn't catch you over
all this noise.

Catherine: I said I'm not on your team.

Colonel: And why would that be?

Catherine: There is not one piece of factual information
in your speech. You spread hate and lies, and worst of all fear. You
manipulate good men and women into risking their livelihood. And
for what? Your crusade against democracy. You said you respected
me because I told you the truth and not just things you want to hear.
Well this is the price you pay for making such a wish.

BEAT.

BEAT.

Colonel: I was warned not to trust you. You Catholics are all alike. You are whores of Babylon. You can't be trusted because you have strayed from the true Christian light. You have allowed yourself to be tainted by the mud races. Your race should be your religion. Going against your race is treason, and we know how to deal with that. When the cleansing comes, you will be first.

The Colonel spits on Catherine. And begins to walk away. With his back towards her, he stops in his tracks when she calls out his real name. He never turns to face her.

Catherine: Bill Davidson. I won't stop until you're behind bars, if it's the last thing I ever do.

Colonel: Don't   make   promises   you   can't keep, you Bitch.

With that he is swallowed by the crowd and she is left there in the aftermath of the chaos.

SCENE TWENTY

Catherine bursts into the FBI office where agents are all floating around their desks.

Catherine: Special Agent Jones.

Jones: Catherine.

Catherine: I'll do whatever you need me to do to
bring down Bill.

Jones: Glad to have you on board, Miss Reilly.

Catherine: Full disclosure, I can't be your woman
on the inside.

Jones: You just said/

Catherine: Let's just say he's been made aware that he
and I will never play on the same team.

Jones: Right. Well, let's get you set up and see how much you learned on your adventure on the farm.

Catherine follows Jones off stage.

SCENE TWENTY ONE

Catherine enters the church in search of Father Paul.

Catherine: Father Paul, I need to make a confession.

Seeing the strain in Catherine he escorts her into his office and shuts the door behind them.

Ft. Paul: What troubles you, Catherine?

Catherine: Forgive me, Father. I didn't listen to your advice, I have gotten myself in too deep.

Ft. Paul: Is this about the trial I've been reading about?

Catherine: I agreed to be the key witness. I thought I could do this, I thought I was strong enough to stand up to him, to take him down. To make him pay for all the pain and suffering he's caused.

Ft. Paul: What is it, Catherine? What's happened?

Catherine: At first it was just small things. The back gate would be opened even though I know I latched it. The phone would ring off the hook in the middle of the night until I had to unplug it. Then it escalated. I came home last week, and my dog was missing. I spent two hours out running around the neighborhood just looking for him.

Ft. Paul: My girl. What have you gotten yourself into?

Catherine: An awful mess, Father. See, I found him, out by the dump and I sent him off to stay with a friend. But then they smashed my windows out while I was at work a few days ago and now… *(can barely speak she is beside herself)* and now, I've just come home to these.

Catherine holds out a manila envelope. Father Paul takes it from her hands, opening up the lip and slipping black and white photos out. Realization dawning on him.

Ft. Paul: These are of your Mother, and your Aunt. And me…

Catherine: It's a warning. If I don't drop out of this trial, you'll all be next. And I cannot have that on my conscience, Father. I also cannot let him win.

Ft. Paul: This isn't a game of Monopoly, Catherine. This is life or death and you made a promise to me, which is akin to a promise to God himself that you would not go this far.

Catherine: I know, Father, but I cannot live with myself if I backed out now and he went free and more innocent people got hurt because of it. I'm sure God can understand my struggle and see that I must complete my mission.

Ft. Paul: This is serious business, Catherine… I'm not sure what you want me to say?

Catherine: I don't want you to say anything. Not now.

I will ask for yours and God's forgiveness when this is all over.
For now, I've come to say goodbye.

Ft. Paul: Goodbye? I don't understand.

Catherine: I'm leaving.

Ft. Paul: When?

Catherine: Right now.

Ft. Paul: Where are you going?

Catherine: Probably some hole in the wall motel.

Ft. Paul: You mean witness protection?

Catherine: It's the only thing I can think of that will
keep you all safe, and allow me to see this to the end.

Ft. Paul: Catherine/

Catherine: Please don't try and talk me out of this.

Ft. Paul: I wasn't, I was just going to say this. Keep your head down, be smart and please, stay safe.

Catherine: I promise, swear on my life this time. I will see you when this is all over.

They hug each other tightly. Before she exits he calls out to her.

Ft. Paul: One moment.

He crosses over to her and places prayer beads in her hand.

Catherine: Thank you, Father.

Ft. Paul: Something tells me you'll be needing these more.

They hug one more time before she exits.

SCENE TWENTY TWO

Catherine is dressed in one of her many courtroom suits. She passes back and forth outside the courtroom doors. She checks her watch and lets out a deep exhale. Suddenly the doors to the courtroom creak open and Jones sticks her head out.

Jones:　　　　　　It's time.

Catherine turns on her heels and follows Jones into the courtroom and walks to the witness stand where a bailiff holds out a bible before her.

Judge:　　　　　　Miss Reilly, please put your hand on the bible. Do you solemnly swear that the evidence you shall give be the truth, the whole truth, and nothing but the truth?

Catherine:　　　　I do.

Catherine takes the stand.

Judge: The defence may begin.

Suddenly The Colonel stepped out from behind his desk and began walking over to the witness stand.

Lawyer: Objection, your honour! He's trying to intimidate the witness.

Judge: Sustained. Mr. Davidson, if you insist on questioning the witness yourself, which I strongly discourage, you must do so at the safe distance of lectern, and that you may not approach the witness without expressed permission.

Colonel: Of course, your honour. I wouldn't want to intimidate the witness in any way. Miss Reilly, it says here that you claim that none of the farmers who used my sight draft loans were able to save their farms.

Catherine: That is correct.

Colonel: And all together how many farms have you been able to save through mediation and restructuring?

Catherine: I have participated in over 300 mediations, and have been able to save everyone of those farms, except one.

Colonel: And why exactly was that?

Catherine: He simply didn't want to farm anymore.

Colonel: So it wasn't a lack of effort or knowledge?

Catherine: I assure you it was neither.

Colonel: And what proof do you have for the courthouse today that would show that you would be incapable of replicating that success with my VA loan repayment option?

Catherine: Mr. Davidson, what you are offering is not a financial benefit to any farmer with a VA loan. Your information that the government will take care of missing or defaulted VA loans is at best mistaken, and at worst costing people not only their livelihoods but their actual life.

Colonel: What proof do you have of that?

Catherine: Mr. Avery. He committed suicide when the bank repossessed his family farm after halting all payments to his VA loan on behest of you telling him that the government would cover the cost of the loan.

Colonel: I did not slip the noose around his neck. I did not force Mr. Avery to jump. In fact I cannot even be held accountable for being the one who stopped payments to the VA on behalf of Mr. Avery. We are all born with our own free will, and Mr. Avery simply executed that right, until the very end.

Catherine: You are correct in that logic, Mr. Davidson. However, it is your name all over the loan documents that state the false information of the repatriation of the loans in question. So, you may not have been the one to forcibly sign Mr. Avery's name to the false documentation in which he believed he was secured by the government for the outstanding loan payments, you may not have tied the rope, or pushed him off with your own hands. But you and I, and now the jury, as well, know that you are the only one to blame for this loss of land and life.

The courtroom erupts and the Judge bangs their gavel several times.

Judge: There will be order in my courtroom. Mr. Davidson, if you have no further questions, and the prosecution has no questions to add, I suggest we recess for the day.

Lawyer: We are satisfied, your Honour.

The Colonel just nods in aggravated defeat. And the courtroom begins to empty. FBI agent Jones saddles up next to Catherine.

Jones: Very "you know nothing about the truth."

Catherine: Thank you, Agent Jones. Glad I could be of help today.

Jones: Would you like me to escort you back to the motel or would you like to stop and get dinner on the way?

Catherine: If it's all the same to you, Agent Jones, I think I'd like to sleep in my own bed tonight.

Jones: Catherine, this isn't over.

Catherine: I know. But all those intimidation tactics were to keep me from testifying, and I just did that.

Jones: Men like Davidson aren't just going to take today with a grain of salt.

Catherine: I don't think he'll be a problem anymore.

Jones: Okay. I can spare an agent for the night.

Catherine: I appreciate it, Agent Jones. On the way back, do you mind if we make a stop to pick up my dog?

They both exit the courtroom.

SCENE TWENTY THREE

It's a giant church picnic. Father Paul and Catherine are catching amongst the crowd.

Ft. Paul: Is it all over?

Catherine: Just the first part. We have him nailed
on his financial dealings with the government. Later comes the
criminal aspect.

Ft. Paul: Will it be back to witness protection
for you then?

Catherine: No, I think we've seen the last of his
intimidation tactics. I feel I've proven they don't work on me.

Ft. Paul: It's so good to have you back, Catherine. I
really missed you, we all really missed you.

Just then someone in the crowd chants
SING FOR US CATHERINE.

Catherine: No, I couldn't possibly.

Ft. Paul: The church choir really hasn't been the
same without you. How about just one song?

The crowd cheers and chants.

Catherine: Okay, okay. Just one song.

She sets down her plate and makes her way to the front of the picnic. She begins to sing "Old Rugged Cross." Fade to Black.

SCENE TWENTY FOUR

Catherine sits at her desk as a co-worker knocks on her door.

Co-Worker: Happy Valentine's Day, Catherine, have any plans for tonight?

Catherine: Just some take out and more case files. The stack seemed to have multiplied by ten since I've been gone.

Co-Worker: It is so nice to have you back. This place just isn't the same without you. Anyway, I have to head out. I don't want to keep Dawn waiting any longer than I have to. Have a great night, Catherine.

She waves goodbye as the Co-Worker exits. She continues reading a file for a couple beats, then blows out the breath she was holding, checks her watch and starts gathering case files and placing them into her briefcase. She stands and stretches before grabbing her coat off the rack and heading to the office door. She puts the key in the lock to close up for the night when a figure steps out of the shadows and attacks her.

Attacker: An eye for an eye saith the Lord.

He swings a knife at Catherine and she's able to block it with her hand. Blood begins to flow from her eye.

Attacker: This is for The Colonel, you bitch!

He begins to swing again but she catches him up. She begins to fight back, punching and swinging. She lets out a guttural scream.

Catherine: What do you want from me!

He spits at her, knocking her back, they are separated for a brief moment. He lets out a cold vile laugh.

Attacker: You betrayed your race. You sided with the Jew Government. You deserve to pay for your betrayal.

This time she sees him lunge, she is ready. She uses the momentum to knee him in the groin. He crashes to his knees in pain and she begins to run. The attacker gets up, closing the distance between them in a few giant strides and lunges for her. The lights go up and down, as if someone is watching the scene play out of a blinking eye. Catherine's voice is heard as a voice over on top of the snippets of scenes of the continuing attack we see in the flashes of light.

Cath V.O.:   I realized too late that in my attempt to flee I had found myself at the top of the marble staircase. I braced for impact as I watched his red raged face caked in sweat lunge for me. The serenity of falling through time and space is all that I can remember. I thought of Alice as she tumbled down the rabbit hole to Wonderland. What would be waiting for me at the bottom of the stairs? Death? Almost certainly. Still, as my body skipped like a rock down the cold hard stairs, being sent airborne for different lengths of time, all I could think about was Alice and her white Rabbit. Had the Colonel been my White Rabbit? Or was he the Queen of Hearts, sending his dutiful henchman to paint the town red with my blood, as a warning for anyone who dared to stand against him. I remember only snippets of that hour. I remember reaching the bottom like a great wave breaking on the beach, laying their immobile. I remember him kneeling on top of me and spitting out *(the Attacker on stage says his line)* "Repent for your sins and I will spare your life. Do you want to burn in the crimson fire? You have been judged by the brotherhood." A hot and heavy garble of laughter built inside me as I replied *(Catherine on stage pinned beneath the attacker speaks, not the voice over)* "My only judge is Jesus Christ." *(back to voice over)* Faced with certain death, all I knew was to cling hard and strong to my beliefs. No one could take that away from me, not even at the very end. I remember his warm calloused hands pressed against either side of my skull and the pressure of it being plunged into the concrete floor. Then I felt nothing. I could only hear my father, clear as day. He said *(father's voice over)* "Be strong, my girl. Say the Lord's prayer with me." *(Catherine speaks again)* All I could remember was the first verse, so I spoke it word for word with my father, and I waited for the end.

She repeats the first verse of the Lord's prayer again and again and again. After a few blinks of the lights the attacker is gone, the lights slowly fade into just a single spot light. The same image as the opening scene lays out. The sound of a vacuum begins to play. The opening scene repeats itself, the woman rushing in, sending the cleaner to call 911 and holding Catherine saying the Lord's prayer with her, getting the second verse out for her.

ACT TWO

SCENE ONE

Catherine lays in a hospital bed. Machines hooked up to every inch of her body. Father Paul is asleep at the end of her bed, bent over with his arms folded over her leg. She wakes up and looks around. She touches her face and winces in pain. Her hand is wrapped up in bandages and the blood is beginning to come through a bit. The move wakes up Father Paul, who doesn't fully realize that Catherine is conscious. When he notices, in fact she is awake, he jumps to his feet and moves to the head of the bed.

Ft. Paul: You're awake! Catherine, my dear, you're awake.

He silently begins to sob.

Catherine: How do I look?

Ft. Paul: *(Barks out a laugh through a sob)* Horrible. Your one eyeball is firming fixed taking in your ear.

They both try and laugh.

Catherine: What about the man who attacked me?

Silence fell. BEAT.

Ft. Paul: He got away, Catherine. The cleaning lady found you at the bottom of the stairs. No one knows for sure how long you'd been like that. I hate to ask you, but… do you remember anything?

Catherine: I'm not sure. It's all so fuzzy. Like I'm watching it through TV static, only getting a clear image for a second before it's gone again.

Ft. Paul: Dan was the one who called me. They brought you in and you were so unrecognizable that he only realized it was you once someone brought in your briefcase. He called me straight away.

Catherine: Poor Dan. I forgot he was a police officer.

Ft. Paul: It's a lucky thing that he is. He put down that it was an attempted sexual assault to keep your name and most of the details out of the papers.

Catherine: Well, thank God for that.

Ft. Paul: You know who it was though, Catherine. Don't you?

Catherine: I honestly don't. It wasn't The Colonel, if that's what you mean. It wasn't even that annoying German henchman of his. It's a voice in my mind I can't place.

Ft. Paul: But it had to have been The Colonel who ordered it, so he has to be held responsible for the attack one way or another.

Catherine: What if I can't get the memory of the attack back. What if I can't get my memory back at all?

Ft. Paul: Let's try not to worry about that yet. Let's take it one step at a time.

SCENE TWO

Catherine is out of her bed doing physical therapy, trying to get the hang of walking again. She gets frustrated and collapses back on the bed.

Catherine: This is never going to end, is it?

Doctor: Catherine, do you have any idea how lucky you are to even be alive, let alone up and walking around?

Catherine: You call that walking? I've seen babies crawl further and faster than that.

Doctor: Need I remind you that you very easily could have been in a wheelchair the rest of your life?

Catherine: Please don't tell me to take it one step at a time. I've been here for over a month now, and that's all anyone keeps saying to me! "Don't worry, Catherine, your memory will slowly start coming back to you, just take it one step at a time." "You're doing great Catherine, just one step at a time."
 I get it, I get it!

Doctor: I think you need to give yourself some grace. A terrible, life changing event took place for you, without your consent. And now you are paying dearly for it. I think the very least you can do, is cut yourself some slack and celebrate even the smallest of victories. Sure, they may be a far cry from the victories you are used to celebrating; but Catherine, whether you like it or not, this is your new reality. So get with the program, or you will drive yourself insane.

Catherine: That's some tough love there, Doctor.

Doctor: You're a tough woman, Catherine.
Don't forget that.

Catherine: I might need to tattoo it on my arm if I don't start getting my memory back soon.

Doctor: All in good time. Have you started to think long term? About what you plan on doing to care for yourself if your memory doesn't fully come back? We have warned you that it may not.

Catherine: Father Paul has suggested therapy, but I'm just not sold. Why bother harping on the past that I can't even remember fully.

Doctor: It might be best to heed his advice on this one. Even if you never remember a single detail about that night, your body will. Our muscles store trauma like muscle memory. The more you begin to get back to your natural physical rhythm, the more that trauma will work its way out. It's better to have a plan in place than be caught off guard with no one to help you through it.

Catherine: I'll look into it. Now, can you please help me up? I'd like to try and make it down the hall and back today and I'll never get there if I stay in this bed talking about my feelings.

Doctor: If you want out of your bed, you can get yourself out.

The Doctor flashes a cheeky smile as Catherine grins from ear to ear. She loves the challenge. She fights to get herself out of the bed and onto her feet. She slowly begins to make her way off stage with the Doctor walking backwards watching her as they exit.

SCENE THREE

Catherine sits at the FBI table. FBI agent Jones stairs into the mirrored wall.

Jones: I wish I had better news for you, Catherine. You deserve more.

BEAT.

Catherine: I don't understand…

Jones: With your memory/

Catherine: No, I understand that. What I don't understand is how my previous testimony just gets discarded like trash. There was nothing wrong with my brain then.

Jones: It's just the way it works.

Catherine: Everything was for nothing then. I got my skull bashed in for nothing. I was stabbed repeatedly for nothing. I worked hard on my recovery for nothing.

Jones: The system failed you. For that there are no words to express my deepest regret.

Catherine: Now what? He wins?

Jones: We can still move forward with the trial, just not with you.

Catherine: So I'm just a discarded pawn to you?

Jones: I don't know what else to say…

Catherine: How about, 'THANK YOU, CATHERINE.' How about, 'don't worry, Catherine, I'll fight the system Catherine, I'll make sure your sacrifice wasn't in vain, Catherine.'

Jone: I am sorry Catherine, but there's nothing else I CAN DO. No matter how much I wish there was.

Jones turns and exits the room without another word.

SCENE FOUR

Catherine hobbles to a table with her leg in a brace and crutches under each arm. She carries a tray in one hand and maneuvers the crutches one at a time. She plunks herself down at the table out of breath and starts setting up to eat.
A woman slides in next to her.

Molly: It's you.

Catherine: Excuse me?

Molly: I'm Molly Asher.

Catherine: I'm sorry Molly, have we met before? Your voice, it sounds familiar.

Molly: Yes. Well, no. Not really. I was the one who stayed with you when the ambulance came.

Catherine: You…

Molly: I'm sorry, this is very rude of me.

Molly gets up to leave. Catherine catches her hand.

Catherine: Thank you.

Molly: I'm just so glad to see you. After they took you away, well, there was no way for me to know if you'd made it or not. I kept telling myself you had, that somehow I'd have felt it in my bones if you'd gone.

Catherine: You're the only one who knows what happened to me that day. You and one other person outside of law enforcement.

Molly: And the cleaning woman that found you.

Catherine: Poor woman.

Molly: She came running into my office screaming bloody murder. Eventually she gave up trying to speak and just tugged me along down the hall. No one in your office knows what's happened?

Catherine: Not even my own family.

Molly: You've gone through all this on your own?

Catherine: It's better that way. Why make more people suffer than absolutely necessary.

Molly: You are a lot stronger than me.

Catherine: I'm less convinced these days that strength has anything to do with it. I think it's more sheer stubbornness, if I'm at all honest.

Molly: Can I ask you a question?

Catherine: Of course.

Molly: What's your name? I'd like to be able to add your name to the prayer I say for you each night.

Catherine: My name is Catherine.

Molly: It's nice to meet you, Catherine.

Catherine: It's an honour to meet you, Molly.

Molly: I just did the Christian thing to do.

Catherine: This is going to sound like a bizarre question, I still don't remember anything from that day. But, did you...say the Lord's Prayer with me?

Molly: Yes! You just kept repeating the first verse, and so, I said the ending for you, over and over again. You'd start, and I'd finish.

Catherine: I heard you. I thought you were an angel.

Molly: I'm no angel.

Catherine: To me you are.

Molly: I can't tell you how happy I am to see you here.

Catherine: It's all because you got me here.

Molly: So no one at your office knows what happened?

Catherine: No, they think I finally cashed in all my vacation days and took an extended holiday. If only.

Molly: And your leg?

Catherine: I told them I hurt it on vacation. They are so used to my old sports injuries acting up, that for the few people who did ask about it, no one seemed to have reason to think I'd lie.

Molly: Did they, you know…

Catherine: Catch him?

Molly: Yes.

Catherine: No. No one saw him, I can't remember much more than his voice… there wasn't a lot to go off of.

Molly: What would make someone do something so horrible?

Catherine: I tried to put away a bad man, he was harming good people and I was a witness to it, and he tried to make it go away.

Molly: Wait…are you talking about the Bill Davidson trial?

Catherine: Yes, how did you guess that?

Molly: My husband…he's working on the trial. Just a legal assistant for the prosecution, but he mentioned something about the lead witness. He mentioned you. Well, not by name of course, but it's you.

Catherine: That would be me. Did he…has he mentioned anything else about the trial?

Molly: Not much. Just how angry he is at our judicial system. How there should have been more done to protect you, and how he's no longer as positive about the outcome.

Catherine: But they are still moving on with the trial?

Molly: Oh, yes! I guess after you testified it empowered a few farmers to come forward themselves.

Catherine: Did he happen to mention their names?

Molly: Unfortunately, no. He only tells me as much as he can get away with.

Catherine: I see. Well, it gives me some piece of mind knowing that I haven't cost them the entire trial.

Molly: Desperate men do desperate things, Catherine. He knew you had him on the ropes. I know it's no consolation, but know that you made that man fear womankind. Which, by the sounds of it, is something he's not used to.

Catherine: Hey Molly, would you like to have lunch again this week? I can't tell you what a burden it's been to go through this alone. I didn't realize how nice it would be to have someone to talk to who knew what happened.

Molly: It would be my pleasure.

Molly and Catherine grin ear to ear and they go about eating their lunches in comfortable silence.

SCENE FIVE

Inside a courtroom, Catherine stands sans crutches in a suit. She is back practicing law. The Judge bangs his gavel and everyone takes their seat.

Judge: Ms. Reilly, you may begin your cross examination when you are ready.

Catherine rises, documents in hand and strides towards the witness.

Catherine: Ms. Parker, you claim that you would never intentionally put your daughter in harm's way.

Def. Lawyer: Objection, your Honour, leading the witness.

Judge: Overruled. Please answer, Ms. Parker.

Parker: Of course I wouldn't.

Catherine: So, you'd never let little Gloria play out in the streets unattended, or leave opened cleaning products out within her reach?

Parker: Of course not!

Catherine: Then answer us this one question, Ms. Parker. Why is it that you are allowing your daughter to live under the same roof as a known pedophile?

Parker: I didn't know.

Catherine: But when you were made aware by my client, Dorothy Adler - Gloria's grandmother, of your partner's previous arrest record, you made no efforts to remove him from your lives. In fact, you wouldn't even let Dorothy take Gloria out of the house.

Parker: I thought she was lying.

Catherine: And now that you know Mrs. Adler's claims to be true, may I ask where your partner is currently?

Ms Parker remains silent.

Judge: Answer the question, Ms. Parker.

Parker: He no longer lives with us.

Catherine: Is it not true that he remains in contact with you, and with Gloria?

Def. Lawyer: Objection. There is no proof that my client remains in contact with her ex.

Catherine: There is, your Honour. I'd like to submit to the jury *(just then Catherine's leg locks up as she takes a step forward causing her to drop all her papers)* Forgive me, your Honour, just a moment.

She painfully bends down to start putting together all the notes. She is scrambling.

Judge: Are we about ready to continue, Ms Reilly?

Catherine: Yes, your Honour. Now as I was saying,
Mrs. Adler, there is proof here I'd like to submit/

Judge: You mean there is proof you'd like to
submit against Ms Parker.

Catherine: Yes… against Ms Parker… on behalf of
Mrs. Adler.

Judge: Counselor, are you fit to move
forward today?

Catherine: *(Frantically flipping through her notes that
are out of order)* Yes, your Honour, I just need a moment to get
my notes in order.

Judge: I move that we take a recess for the
remainder of the day, and that we reconvene tomorrow at ten am.

The judge bangs his gavel and everyone rises while he exits.
Catherine grabs her belongings from her desk, gives a reassuring
squeeze to Dorothy Adlers arm, and they exit the courtroom.

SCENE SIX

It's a busy restaurant. A man in a sharply dressed suit sits sipping
a cocktail alone at a table. A frantic Catherine limps in
to join him.

Catherine: I'm so sorry I'm late, Jim.
Parking was a nightmare.

Jim: No worries. Thank you for meeting
with me, Catherine.

Catherine: I was thrilled that you called. It's been
ages. I haven't seen you since after our final bar exam. How has
everything been going? I heard you're actually a member of the
Bar Association now! Small world.

Jim: I am. That's actually why I wanted to meet with you. I felt a sense of obligation to you, for our old school days. I always rather looked up to you Catherine.

Catherine: This isn't a social visit, is it Jim?

Jim: I'm afraid not.

Catherine: They want to take my license away, don't they?

Jim: I convinced them to let me talk to you first. To let me beseech you to resign on your own terms.

Catherine: Except it won't be on my own terms, now, will it?

Jim: Don't let them drag your reputation through the mud, Catherine. It isn't worth it.

Catherine: Is there any other way?

Jim: I am allowed to make you one offer. You can continue to practice law, but you will never be allowed to return to a courtroom.

Catherine: Why don't you just cut me off at the knees.

Jim: There are plenty of lawyers who never go to trial, Catherine.

Catherine: This can't be because of the Parker/Adler trial.

Jim: It's the root of it.

Catherine: I came back the next day and won that case. Gloria is now safe with her Grandmother and no harm came from it.

Jim: You aren't as sharp as you once were. Ever since you came back from your "vacation" you haven't been the same. You're more forgetful, you're easily thrown off during questioning. Did you not think we'd notice that you've gone from memorizing every single detail of your case to holding cue cards in your hand?

Catherine: Just tell me, was it my own
clients that complained?

Jim: No. It's the Judges.

Catherine: Then there's no fighting this. My only
option is to be a lawyer who doesn't practice law.

Jim: We aren't taking your license, you can
practice law still. Just, no more trials.

Catherine: And how long will that last before the Bar
Association deems me completely incompetent and comes
for my license?

Jim: Catherine, you are the least incompetent
lawyer I have ever come across. No one is arguing that you are a
fantastic lawyer. Hell, have you ever lost?

Catherine: No.

Jim: So, quit while you're ahead. Keep your reputation intact. Please don't make me have to vote to remove you from the bar.

Catherine: Okay…

Jim: I really am sorry, Catherine. I'm not supposed to tell you this, but I heard about what you did. I heard about how you testified in the Bill Davidson trial, so it wasn't hard to put two and two together when we found out about the leading witness of the tragic attack. I just wanted to say this before I go. Thank you. I don't know many white folk who would have been willing to stand up to a white supremacist like you did. Even if it feels like you've been paid back in nothing but unkindness, please know that my world is all the better for your bravery.

With that, Jim stood up, shook Catherine's hand and exited. A waiter showed up and took Catherine's drink order.

Waiter: Will you be staying?

Catherine: Yes, but just for one drink. Can I please get a scotch on the rocks?

Waiter: Certainly.

SCENE SEVEN

An extremely intoxicated Catherine sits at the table explaining away her troubles to a very uncomfortable waiter.

Catherine: And now what do I have? Who am I if I can't enter another courtroom?

Waiter: I'm so sorry, Ma'am, but do you have someone we could call to take you home?

Catherine: Nope. I'm all alone. Just how I like it. I'm a very private person, you know. Maybe too private. If I'd spent half my time trying to do what's expected of me as a woman and settled down and got married and had kids, maybe then I'd still be able to practice law in a courtroom. Maybe then I wouldn't have gone chasing after the White Rabbit.

Waiter: You're sure there's no one I can call for you?

Catherine: Can you call my Father? Well, he's not MY Father. But he's my Father. Father Paul.

Waiter: Do you have his number?

Catherine: Yup. *She sloppily takes the waiter's pen and pad and scribbles the number down.*

Waiter: I'll be back.

Catherine: And this is how my cookie crumbles.

Just then Father Paul enters the restaurant. He looks around for her and marches over to the table.

Ft. Paul: Oh Catherine.

Catherine: Father Paul! You're here. How did you get here?

Ft. Paul: The waiter called me. Said one of my
children needed my help and I came. Never did I think it
would be you.

Catherine: Are you disappointed in me, Father?

Ft. Paul: No. Just concerned.
Catherine, what's happened?

Catherine: I've been stripped of my right to practice
law in a courtroom. I'm just a paper pusher lawyer now.

Ft. Paul: I hadn't realized it had gotten so bad.

Catherine: It's my brain. I just can't keep information
in there the way I used to.

Ft. Paul: Maybe this is for the best. A little less stress
in your life could only do you good at this point, Catherine.

Catherine: Did you know that I was the first in my
graduating class to get published in the Bar Journal? I was first to
become an ATLA member, the first to win a court case. Now I'm
the first to retire.

BEAT.

Ft. Paul:　　　　　Let's get you home, Catherine. A good night's rest can make anything better.

Catherine:　　　　　What's a good night's rest? I don't think I've had one in months.

Father Paul helps Catherine to her feet. Drops some cash on the table and helps her exit the stage.

SCENE EIGHT

Catherine is at home in her bed. She has the side table lamp on, and all you can hear is the clicking of the clock on the wall. She begins to jiggle her legs. Soon she throws back the covers and begins to limp back and forth. She rubs at her knee. Her eyes. She holds her hand up to the light studying the scare. The attacker's voice rings out in the silence.

V.O.:   An eye for an eye the Lord saith.

She covers her ears and continues pacing back and forth.

V.O.:   You deserve to pay for your betrayal.

She begins to get more agitated. The clock ticking is getting louder and louder.

V.O: Repent for your sins.

She lets out a blood curdling scream as she runs over to the clock and rips it from the wall and throws it, crashing to the ground. She melts to the floor herself racked with sobs.

SCENE NINE

Catherine is sitting on a doctor's table. The Doctor from the hospital examines her.

Doctor: Catherine…

Catherine: Please don't start with me. I'm just here to get cleared to continue my work.

Doctor: I can't do that.

Catherine: Please. I've lost so much already, don't take this away from me.

Doctor: I'm not taking away anything from you, Catherine. I just cannot medically clear you to return to work. Not in your condition.

Catherine: I'm fine!

Doctor: No you are not! Catherine, you are not the same person you were before. You're probably never going to be that person you were before the attack ever again. I have never sugar coated anything for you in the past, and I refuse to start now. This is what? The fourth check up since I released you. Every time you come into my office you are more stooped over to the right. You seem more confused than the time before, and I'm concerned that you aren't sleeping properly. I don't think I need to tell you how hurt you were, you have all the scars to prove it. There's no shame in admitting that you are disabled. How many disabled people have you helped over the years? They were all at the place you are now. Let me help you.

Catherine: Okay.

Doctor: I'm on your side. I'm not going anywhere.

They hugged and Catherine cried.

SCENE TEN

Catherine walks into the FBI office. Jones spots her and jumps up from her desk.

Jones: Catherine, what are you doing here?

Catherine: I didn't know where else to go. I've been noticing two men in a ford truck, they've been following me around town for days now. I'd bet my life that they are outside right now waiting for me.

Jones: Shit.

Catherine: What's going on?

Jones: We've set a trial date for Bill Davidson's criminal charges.

Catherine: What does that have to do with me? I can't even testify.

Jones: He must know you're still alive.

Catherine: I still don't understand how that plays into the two men who are outside right now following my every move.

Jones: He must think that we've called you to testify against him.

Catherine: That doesn't make any sense! I haven't even been medically cleared to return to work anymore, let alone be a lead witness in a criminal trial.

Jones: Did you say you had to give up work?

Catherine: Yes. Just another thing Bill Davidson has taken from me.

Jones: And have you applied for employment insurance or disability?

Catherine: Yes, why?

Jones: In the past few weeks, how many times have you been in and out of this federal building?

Catherine: I don't know, I'd say at least three times.

Realization dawning on Catherine.

C. Continued: They must think I've been coming here. To work with you on the trial.

Jones: He no doubt thinks you are a key witness.

Catherine: So, what do I do now? If he knows I'm alive, and he thinks I'm working with you on his case, he's not going to take it very well.

Jones: There's only one way to keep you safe, Catherine.

Catherine: No. I said no last time.

Jones: And you almost died, need I remind you.

Catherine: I have enough reminders.

Jones: Catherine, I can't force you into witness protection. And I won't beg you to care more about your own life than I do.

Catherine: I just, I can't imagine leaving behind my life here.

Jones: Not to sound crass, but what life, Catherine? I know you love your church and your friends. But you aren't working, you look like you're falling apart. PTSD is a real condition. I know that we've only just started to name it, but it's written all over you. Think about this as a fresh start. Hopefully it won't be forever. I'm hoping to nail his ass to the wall. For you and for all the farmers he's screwed over.

Catherine: Okay. Can I say goodbye first?

Jones: Yes. Just… don't tell them where you're going.

Catherine: Where am I going?

Jones: How does Florida sound?

Catherine: I've always loved the beach.

SCENE ELEVEN

Catherine enters an empty church. Father Paul is preparing for Sunday Service and he is at the altar going over and fixing part of his sermon. He lights up when he sees Catherine.

Ft. Paul: My dear, it's so good to see you.

Catherine: Hello Father, have I interrupted?

Ft. Paul: You can interrupt me any day but Sunday.

Catherine: That works out well, then.

Ft. Paul: You look…

Catherine: Tired?

Ft. Paul: Worried.

Catherine: I've come to confess something.

Ft. Paul: Of course.

Catherine: Maybe we should sit?

Ft. Paul: Right, of course.

He gestures for her to take a seat in a pew and he sits in the one in front of her and turns back and rests his arm along the backside to face her.

Catherine: I don't even know how to begin. I am so grateful for everything you have done for me. Not just recently, but ever since I came to this parish. I hope you know how much you have changed my life.

Ft. Paul: Of course I do. Catherine, as lovely as this flattery is, you are beginning to worry me and you have exceeded your worry limit for two life times. What is the matter?

Catherine: They have begun the criminal trial for Bill Davidson.

Ft. Paul: I thought you were ineligible to be a witness on the case moving forward.

Catherine: I am.

Ft. Paul: I don't understand…

Catherine: He doesn't seem to know that I can no longer be a key witness.

Ft. Paul: How could he possibly know that information?

Catherine: This morning, and for the past week, I have noticed the same grey pick up truck outside of the federal building downtown. I've been going in there to file my paperwork for my disability claim.

Ft. Paul: Okay?

Catherine: They don't know that though. They see me going into the Federal building again after all this time at the same exact moment the FBI is proceeding with the criminal charges against The Colonel.

Ft. Paul: Catherine, you need to leave.

Catherine: I am.

Ft. Paul: Now I understand.

Catherine: I spoke with Special Agent Jones, they will be moving me out of state indefinitely. I have come to say goodbye, Father.

Ft. Paul: As much as it pains me to see you go, to you being reduced to fleeing your home, I understand. Catherine, my dear, one day I want to be able to do your wedding, I cannot and will not do your funeral. So if you must go, then go.

Catherine: I will miss you more than I have words to say.

Ft. Paul: Am I allowed to know where you are being sent?

Catherine: Florida.

Ft. Paul: Excellent. Then I will picture you tan and happy, but most of all, I'll rest knowing you will be safe and alive.

Catherine: Thank you for everything, Father. You have saved my life in more than one way.

Ft. Paul: It has been the great honour of my life serving you, Catherine.

They embrace and Father Paul cries. They let go of each other and for a moment they stand staring at one another in silence. Communicating a lifetime of gratitude with their eyes. Catherine turns to exit, as Father Paul walks back up to the altar and picks up in his sermon preparations exactly where he left off.

SCENE TWELVE

Catherine walks into an office space, a nun stands behind a desk laughing on the phone and staring out a window with her back to Catherine. She takes her jacket off and takes a seat, setting her bag on the ground. The Nun – Sister Anne – turns to see Catherine

sitting down and says, "Right, well I'm off, she has just arrived."
She bursts out laughing "of course, yes I will tell her. Goodbye
now." And she hangs up the phone and moves around the desk
and takes a seat across from Catherine now.

Sister Anne: Hello, Catherine.

Catherine: Was that Father Paul again?

Sister Anne: It's rude to pry, but yes it was. He wanted
me to pass along that the choir sounds like a flock of squawking
ducks without you.

Catherine: What an unfortunate sound.

Sister Anne: Indeed. So, where would you like
to start today?

Catherine: I started to remember. Well, not everything,
bits and pieces from that night.

Sister Anne: How do you feel about that?

Catherine: At first, I didn't realize I was remembering anything real. I felt that maybe perhaps I was just having those horrible nightmares, but while I was awake. Like a memory that my brain was inventing to fill in the gaps. But then this odd thing happened, unlike any of the times before. With these memories, I was able to feel them connect to the memories in my body.

Sister Anne: Did you experience physical pain with the memories?

Catherine: Not pain no. More like a low vibrational humming. As if my body was confirming that these memories were in fact real memories.

Sister Anne: What did you experience after you realized that you were recalling events from that night?

Catherine: This is going to sound bizarre.

Sister Anne: Catherine you have been coming to these counselling sessions for over six months, you should know by now there is very little in the way of confessions that would shock me.

Catherine: Well, I just sat there and "watched" it like a movie. A very short and yet somehow endlessly long, glitchy movie that was stuck on a loop.

Sister Anne: What happened once the movie in your mind came to an end?

Catherine: I sat down, and I wrote it all out. Every last detail I could salvage.

Sister Anne: How did that make you feel? To put down those details into words, to read them back and see them in black and white.

Catherine: Truthfully, it felt like a relief. I remembered. Not everything, but that means my brain must be healing. Something no one 'till now knew for certain would ever happen.

Sister Anne: There is so very little in the way of certainty when it comes to brain injuries. It makes me very excited to hear that, no matter how brutal it would have been to experience it all again, that you were able to remember something from that night.

Catherine:　　　　Sister Anne, this may be too much to ask for, but would you mind if I read it to you? I was curious to see what might come of saying the words out loud, and well, I couldn't bring myself to read them out alone.

Sister Anne:　　　　Yes, of course, I think hearing and saying the words that you wrote from your own memory of the worst night of your life.. Well, it might be the first tangible piece of closure you will have gotten from the entire experience.

Catherine:　　　　I hope so.

She begins to dig in her bag for her leather bound journal and she pulls it out and opens it to the page. Her breath is suddenly stuck in her lungs.

Sister Anne:　　　　It's okay, Catherine. You're safe, you're here with me. The words are in the past. Take a deep breath, and begin.

Catherine takes a large gulp of air and begins reading.

Catherine: I remember that morning the air was crisp, I had taken my dog out for a walk around the lake and I remember taking in large gulps of air and thinking to myself how beautiful it was. If I had known then that would be the last time I could do something so simple, I'd not have rushed him to do his business and get home. The work day passed like any other. The stack of cases on my desk somehow managed to get larger despite being able to close some out. I was the last to lock up, there was nothing unusual about that. There is a gap in my memory still, but I can see myself putting the key into the lock, not thinking of the importance of having checked my surroundings. I can see myself from the perspective of a fly on the way. The man swings at me, my glasses go flying down the hall. Blood begins to pour out of the wound above my right eye and trickle into it. I haven't registered that I've been cut by a knife. I haven't registered that I'm in a fight for my life. I am sore and confused and I can hardly see. I can see myself being stabbed. A slash to my wrist, and a through and through into my hand. I see that even though I am wounded I still manage to fight back. I have him up against the wall now and I am punching him, I don't remember doing that. I don't remember overpowering him. I can see that my knuckles are cut and bleeding now, and I realize that he must have been wearing braces, and that is what destroyed my knuckles. There is a moment of hesitation on my end, and he reaches up and grabs my neck. His fingers squeeze tightly making it hard to breathe. I managed to give him another good shove into the wall and connect my knee into his abdomen. He lets me go, and that's when I run. I knew that I had fallen from the top of the staircase, but I never had the image of it in my mind. The way my body bounced and cracked on each step. I never knew what happened after that, until last night. I saw him run down the stairs after me, picking up his knife that had tumbled down the steps with me. He began screaming at me, threatening me with my faith. He stepped on my shoulder and I felt a searing hot white pain as I listened to the bones crunch beneath it. I saw him bend down to his knee and plunge the knife into my body again and again. I could feel each stab wound tingle in my now healing body in acknowledgement that this was real. I saw him, in a rage and still deeply unsatisfied by my unwillingness to submit to him, pick up my skull in both his hands and ram it into the ground over and over. I counted with the sound of each thwack on the concrete until the number got too high to stomach or comprehend. After what seemed like a lifetime I gave into the darkness.

BEAT.

BEAT.

BEAT.

Sister Anne: You have probably heard enough sympathies to last you into the next life, so I will spare you mine. I will, however, say this, Catherine. What happened to you was and will never be your fault. There is nothing you could have done differently to prevent such an atrocious act of violence from happening to you. I say this because if there was something that could have been done, that would have involved a set of logical circumstances, and there is absolutely nothing logical about what that man did. I know it's one thing to sit there and nod along as you hear me say this was not your fault, that you are not to blame, and another thing entirely to sit there and nod along as I say these things and truly understand and believe them. You have come such a long way in your healing process, Catherine, you have just started to reclaim what was taken from you. So now, my only question left for you today is this: What do you plan on doing with your second chance at life?

Catherine sits there silently and chews at her lips absorbing every word deeply into her body. There is a moment before either of them says another word.

Catherine: I want to live my life fully, not just exist.

Sister Anne: Good, good, and how do you plan on doing that?

Catherine: I want to fall in love, and I want to sing in a choir again. I want to stop hiding away for fear of losing it all once more. My biggest fear is, I will get to the end of my life and realize that I died a long time ago, at the bottom of those stairs and I just moved through all those years as a shell of a human being.

Sister Anne: So don't. Go on vacations and sing till your lungs give out. Giving up now and hiding away from what your heart is screaming for, it's just another way that he wins. And Catherine, you have come too far to let him have another ounce of you.

Catherine: Thank you, Sister Anne. I suppose my best revenge is a long life lived to the fullest.

Sister Anne chuckles at this. Catherine places her journal back in her bag and they stand up together, they wordlessly nod their goodbyes and Catherine exits. Black out.

SCENE THIRTEEN

The stage is black, Catherine is but a voice off stage.

V.O. Cath: When you're first learning to hit a curveball the hardest thing to do is stay in the batter's box. At first the pitch looks like it is going to hit you. If you bail out of the batter's box, it may still curve across the plate for a strike. If you stay put, it might hit you, but even if it does, it won't hurt as bad as a fastball can. You have to overcome your fear of the pain, stay in the box, wait for the pitch to finish, and then hit the stuffing out of it. Learning to be patient and not to fear pain takes a lifetime to master, and sometimes, you have to take one for the team.

The lights slowly begin to come up on a choir. Catherine stands centre stage and she begins to sing Amazing Grace and the Choir joins in and they sing the song out.

END.